*for my wonderful agent, Helen
and my dear parents.*

Lincoln Children's
First Editions

Brimming with creative inspiration, how-to projects, and useful information to enrich your everyday life, Quarto Knows is a favourite destination for those pursuing their interests and passions. Visit our site and dig deeper with our books into your area of interest: Quarto Creates, Quarto Cooks, Quarto Homes, Quarto Lives, Quarto Drives, Quarto Explores, Quarto Gifts, or Quarto Kids.

The Best Sound in the World © 2018 Quarto Publishing plc.
Text & Illustrations © 2018 Cindy Wume
First published in 2018 by Lincoln Children's Books, an imprint of The Quarto Group.
The Old Brewery, 6 Blundell Street, London N7 9BH, United Kingdom.
T (0)20 7700 6700 F (0)20 7700 8066 www.QuartoKnows.com

The right of Cindy Wume to be identified as the author and illustrator of this work has been asserted by her in accordance with the Copyright, Designs and Patents Act, 1988 (United Kingdom).

A catalogue record for this book is available from the British Library.

ISBN 978-1-78603-169-3

The illustrations were created in gouache, coloured pencil and ink
Set in Brandon Grotesque

Published by Rachel Williams and Jenny Broom
Designed by Zoë Tucker
Edited by Katie Cotton
Production by Jenny Cundill and Kate O'Riordan

Manufactured in Guangdong, China CC052018

1 3 5 7 9 8 6 4 2

Roy was a little lion
who lived in the big city.
His favourite thing was music.

Next door to
Roy lived Jemmy,
a lemur who liked
music too.

Whenever Roy played,
Jemmy would be there,

dancing,

clapping,

and singing along.

It was very distracting,
for someone who was going
to be a great musician.

"To be a famous violinist," thought Roy, "first I need to find beautiful sounds."

So Roy spent hours listening for different noises and putting them in little bottles.

But when he tried to copy the sounds on his violin, none of them sounded quite beautiful enough.

Jemmy tried to find sounds too,

but a great musician doesn't need any help.

The next day, Roy set off on his own
to find the most beautiful sound
in the world.

Roy
went to
the forest
where he
collected
the *plip-plop*
of the rain.

Potter

Pling

pitter

Patter

plong

pling

Roy trekked the
highest mountains
where he collected
the *twitter-tweet*
of the birds.

Twitter

twitter

chitter

Tweet

Roy went to the desert where he collected the *wooooooo* of the whistling wind,

took a rest by the seaside where he found the *splish-splosh* of the tide,

and visited the souk at sunrise to catch the *chitter-chatter* of the market.

Roy went everywhere.

But the more he searched,
the more confused he felt.
Which was the most
beautiful sound?

He couldn't tell.
And everyone he asked
had a different answer.

Roy became more
and more lonely...

So he decided to go home.

When Roy got home everything was the same. He still hadn't found the most beautiful sound in the world, and he was very sad.

Not long after, there was a knock on the door.
It was Jemmy, who tried hard to cheer him up.

He played some tricks,
but they weren't very funny.

He did a silly dance,
but it was really very silly.

Then Jemmy asked Roy to
play the sounds he'd collected
on his journey.

Slowly....

Roy remembered the time he rode the camel in the *woooooo* of the wind.

He remembered playing with the monkey in the *plip-plop* of the rain.

As he remembered the *splish-splosh* of the seaside, he reached for his violin...

But it wasn't there!

Luckily, Jemmy had a surprise for Roy.

As he took back his violin,
Roy realised that Jemmy had been
with him on every step of his journey.

And thinking of his friend,
Roy began to play.

Now Roy and Jemmy
collect noises, together.

In their shop, the people of the city
come to find their favourite sounds.

Sometimes, Roy hears something that makes him want to play his violin. Jemmy is always there, dancing, clapping and singing along.

And it might not be
the most beautiful, but for
Roy it is the best sound
in the world.